HUBBLE BUBBLE

The PESKY PIRATE PRANK!

TRACEY CORDEROY

JOE BERGER

nosy crow

First published in the UK in 2014 by Nosy Crow Ltd
The Crow's Nest, 10a Lant Street
London, SE1 1QR, UK

Nosy Crow and associated logos are trademarks and/or registered
trademarks of Nosy Crow Ltd

3 5 7 9 10 8 6 4

A CIP catalogue record for this book will be available from the British Library.

Printed in Spain

Papers used by Nosy Crow are made from wood grown in
sustainable forests.

ISBN: 978 0 85763 224 1

www.nosycrow.com

CONTENTS

For Charlotte,
with love x
T.C.

For Charlotte,
with love x
J.B.

There was nothing Pandora loved more than spending time with her granny. Araminta Violet Crow was exciting, funny and kind. The only tiny problem was you never quite knew what she'd get up to next. You see, Pandora's granny was (whisper this next bit) … *a witch.*

The PESKY PIRATE PRANK!

Chapter One

"Have some cereal!" Granny grinned as she and Pandora ate breakfast.

Pandora had been staying with Granny all week. They'd been making a costume for Pandora's school play, which was happening today.

Pandora eyed up the box of Froggy-Pops. Breakfast at Granny's was always "different".

In fact, *everything* at Granny's was different. And that's because Pandora's granny was (*whisper it!*) a witch.

Granny tipped some cereal into Pandora's bowl. Phew – it looked normal! But suddenly, as Pandora poured on the milk…

POP!
POP!
POP!

The cereal frogs turned into *real* ones, which went leaping out of the bowl – *ping!*

"I *love* that spell!" giggled Granny. "Such fun!"

Pandora ate some toast instead. As she did, Granny's grandmother clock gave a cough and a door by number eight creaked open. A sleepy little bat came wriggling out, yawning, "School time."

Pandora plodded off upstairs and got into her costume for her school play. She couldn't put it off a moment longer. Then peeping through her fingers, she

looked in the mirror. "Eeek!"

Granny had gone wild when they'd been making this costume. She'd cast every spell on it she knew!

Pandora was meant to be a plain garden slug. Not a slug that twinkled. Not a slug with spinning antennae. And certainly not a slug that blooped out giant rainbow bubbles!

"Splendid!" beamed Granny, zooming in on her broomstick. "Jump on then, Pip dear, and we'll get you to school!"

Pandora gulped. All her friends would *stare*. The Noah's Ark play her class were doing had no mention of super-sparkly slugs!

"Um, Granny," said Pandora slowly, not
wanting to upset her. "I don't think my
teacher likes … *quite* such sparkly slugs."

"Nonsense!" Granny smiled. "You look
magical!"

Pandora sighed. That was the problem! It was clear that Granny had done magic on her costume. But Pandora's parents, who were coming to the play, didn't like magic one bit. Her mum, Moonbeam, was a witch who *never* did magic. And Hugo, her dad, wasn't magical at all, and always said MAGIC led to trouble.

As if this wasn't bad enough, two important "inspector-people" were at school today, too. And Granny was staying to "help" with the play, so *anything* could happen!

Slowly, Pandora climbed on to the broomstick. Then Granny whooshed off up the chimney and out into the sky.

"Ooooh," groaned Pandora, as her costume bubbled wildly. It was going to be another *crazy* day!

Chapter Two

Pandora's teacher was tidying his desk as a herd of animals raced in. And who should be bringing up the rear, but Granny!

"But y-you help on a *Tuesday*," Mr Bibble stuttered. "Just Tuesday! It's *Thursday* today!"

"I'm helping with the play, dear," Granny grinned as Pandora bubbled off to sit by Nellie.

Nellie was dressed as a slug, too. All the animals had to be in pairs like in the real Noah story.

"I wish I looked like you," Nellie whispered.

"Really?" Pandora gasped.

"Can you magic me sparkly, too?" asked Nellie. She knew Pandora, like her granny, was (*whisper it!*) a witch.

"OK," smiled Pandora. "I'll do it at playtime!"

With that, the head
teacher marched in
with two visitors.

"These are the
inspectors!" Mr
Grimly said. "Miss
Froo-Froo and
Mr Splodge."

Miss Froo-Froo
had curly hair,
like a poodle,
and Mr Splodge
looked like a sad
drip of paint.

Mr Grimly marched out and Mr Bibble told the children to go and find their maths books. Then he remembered – *they hadn't tidied their drawers!*

"No!" he shrieked. But it was too late. All the drawers were open wide and children were elbow-deep in dirty tissues, sticky sweets and fallen-out teeth.

Luckily the inspectors hadn't seen, as Granny had kept them talking. Then she secretly flicked her wand, and…

PING!

Suddenly all the maths books were open on the tables and everyone was working quietly.

Mr Splodge looked over.

"Good children!" he said. But Pandora knew Granny's *magic* was to thank for that!

Next, everyone found their model volcanos and tried to make them erupt. Yesterday, when they'd practised this, all the volcanoes had exploded in froth. But today (thanks to Granny) there were no big booms, or giant holes blown in the ceiling.

"Bravo!" barked Miss Froo-Froo. "Just right!"

After play it was painting time
and the children all painted
masterpieces. No drips, no spills,
no messy splatters. Perfect!

Pandora knew that
Granny had
been "helping"
all along. But
the *more* magic
Granny did, the
more excited
she became.

Then, all at
once, she went
too far, and…

SPLAT!!!

A big, black, painty
moustache appeared
under Mr Splodge's
nose.

"Granny!" hissed Pandora.

"Ooops!" Granny whispered. "Must have waved the wand a bit fast!"

Mr Bibble had spotted
the "accident" too. Now
Pandora had to get
Granny away before she
made things even worse.
"Um, Mr Bibble!"
Pandora squeaked.
"Can my granny take
some of us out to
practise our Noah
play?"
"Yes! Good idea!"
Mr Bibble gulped.
"Hurrah!" whooped
Granny wildly.
"To the ark!"

Chapter
Three

Granny and her group burst into the hall.

"*Oh look*," cried Granny, "everything's ready for the play!"

A cardboard-box ark sat on the stage. The children gathered round it. Clover was dressed as Mr Noah, Jake and Bluebell were hippos, and Pandora and Nellie were now both sparkly slugs.

"Can we play in the ark?" Bluebell asked.

"Of course!" Granny smiled. "But let's not play *arks*. Let's play *pirates* instead!"

"Oooh, pirates!" Pandora clapped her hands.

"But the ark doesn't *look* like a pirate ship," said Jake.

"Ah ha!" grinned Granny. "That can be fixed in a jiffy!"

Granny whisked out her wand and uttered the spell…

"*Sparkly treasure and crabs that nip – make this ark a PIRATE SHIP!*"

BANG!

Now the ark was an awesome pirate ship called *The Nipping Crab*. It had a massive cannon, cool ripped sails and a flag with a skull and crossbones on it.

At the top of the mast was a crow's nest *with a real telescope*! And there was rigging to climb and a plank to walk, and the children and Granny were now dressed as pirates.

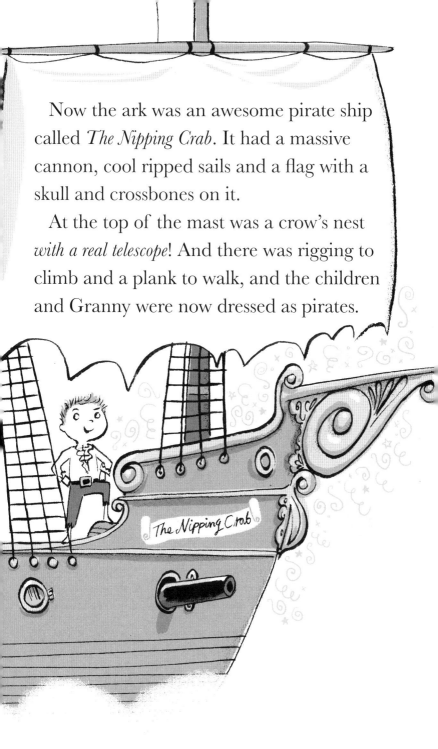

The Nipping Crab

"Let's play a game!"
Captain Granny cried. "I'll
bury some treasure and
you can find it!"

"Yippee!" cheered all the
little pirates.

This sounded
great fun.

Granny waved
her wand and a
beach appeared
with a treasure chest
waiting to be buried.

"Right!" she chuckled. "Set
sail, me hearties!"

Suddenly their ship was on a great big ocean, and off they went at once.

"Wow," cried Pandora, climbing the rigging. "This is cool!"

When they reached the beach, they raced off the ship and started to dig for the treasure. At last Clover found it and they opened the lid.

"Look!" cried Jake. "It's full of coins. *Chocolate* ones!"

They scoffed all the chocolate. But then, sadly, it was time to get back to the classroom.

Granny magicked them out of their pirate clothes.

"Don't forget the ship!" smiled Pandora.

"Oh – but let's leave that as it is," said Granny, covering it with an old curtain. "It looks so much better than the little cardboard ark. Such a lovely surprise at the play this afternoon!"

She said she'd thought of a few more things to liven the play up, too.

"Like what?" asked Pandora, nervously.

"Ahhhh!" grinned Granny. "Just you wait and see!"

Chapter Four

That afternoon the hall was filled with parents, all waiting excitedly for the play.

Mr Bibble led his class on to the stage. "And remember – do *exactly* as I've told you," he whispered.

The inspectors and Mr Grimly were in the front row. Pandora spied her parents there, too.

"OK," said Mr Bibble. He was about to

get things started when Granny whisked the curtain off the pirate ship.

"Oooh!" gasped the crowd. What a surprise! They all thought the *children* had made the ship.

"Gosh!" Miss Froo-Froo smiled. "That's amazing!"

The play began with a worried Mr Noah gazing up at the sky.

"It looks like rain," said Clover timidly.

"*A bit louder, dear,*" whispered Granny.

As Clover opened her mouth again, Granny secretly flicked her wand.

"IT LOOKS LIKE RAIN!" boomed Clover in a giant voice.

With that, all
the animals
piled into
the ship.

They did
it beautifully – no
pushing, no shoving, and
only one needing the toilet.
TICK! TICK! TICK! went the
inspectors' pencils.

Now it was time for the storm. Nellie and Pandora had to make gentle rain sounds on some musical triangles. Then Jake and Bluebell had to shake some shakers as the storm began to rage.

DING! DING! DING! went the triangles. But as they played, Granny secretly waved her wand again, and...

"Oh!" cried Nellie. "*It's really raining! Look!*"

The children looked up. Nellie was right! Real rain was falling from the ceiling. Jake and Bluebell then shook their shakers and the rain got a little heavier.

"*Cool!*" cried a worm, and the parents tittered.

"Oh!" grinned Mr Splodge. "Such wonderful special effects!"

But Mr Grimly knew it was *her. Granny Crow was making this rain!* How many times had he *told* her, *no magic*!

He glared at Granny, who saw him and jumped. As she did, her wand tumbled to the floor shooting out *one last spell* … POP!

Suddenly it was snowing.

"Hooray!" cheered the children. Then the sun came out and a big, bright rainbow appeared over everyone.

"Just like in the Noah story!" smiled the inspectors. "So clever!"

The play ended and Miss Froo-Froo announced that this was the *best* school in town.

"I like it very much!" beamed Mr Splodge.

Pandora liked it, too, especially when Granny helped.

"*Psst – Pandora,*" whispered Granny. "Shall I finish with a tornado? It's one of my best spells, you know!"

"No," smiled Pandora through a sea of blooping bubbles. "Save it for another day, Granny!"

BEDROOMS
&
BROOMSTICKS!

Chapter One

Pandora's parents were going to work and Granny was looking after Pandora.

"Now remember," said Hugo, frowning at Granny, "no m-a-g-i-c."

"We mean it," Moonbeam nodded. "Especially after that bear!"

Yesterday Granny had magicked up a bear in the local

supermarket. This bear had stopped two shifty robbers.

But robbers or not, Moonbeam and Hugo hated magic.

Poor Granny, thought Pandora. No magic today was going to be tricky. Any minute now some builders were coming to build a new bedroom above the garage. And Pandora felt sure that Granny would be *itching* to "help".

Moonbeam and Hugo got into the car.

"Bye then!" Granny called from the door. "And don't you worry – leave everything here to me!"

As soon as they'd gone, Granny raced back inside and whisked out her wand at once.

"*Granny*," gulped Pandora.

"Breakfast!" cried Granny. She waved the wand and...

BANG!

Suddenly the kitchen *exploded* with magic. Granny's cauldron started hissing, the mixer started mixing, knives were chopping, spoons were stirring and rock cakes were baking in the oven.

"Granny, what are you doing?" cried Pandora. "Mum and Dad said no magic!"

"But *breakfast* doesn't count, dear," Granny beamed. "Now, how about some milkshakes!"

With another small wand-flick, the fridge door sprang open and a bottle of milk flew out. It emptied itself into the blender – GLUG, GLUG, GLUG!

Now a handful of strawberries danced from the fruit bowl and went plopping into the milk. Then the blender started to whizz like crazy – DZZZZZZZZZZZZZZ!

As Granny waited, she magicked up some toast and spread it with slimy green jam.

Pandora shuddered. It looked like snot. Ewww!

The blender stopped and Granny poured out the milkshake. It was pink and fluffy and smelled very nice.

"Now for the finishing touch!" Granny smiled.

She spooned something gloopy from her hissing cauldron and dribbled it into the milkshakes. They fizzed, then turned a thick, sludgy blue. "There!" said Granny. "Lovely!"

Suddenly, DING DONG! went the doorbell. Granny hurried over and opened the door, a steaming milkshake in her hand. On the doorstep stood two builders. One was big with giant muscles and one looked like a small, cheerful guinea pig.

"Morning!" smiled Granny. "Here – have a beetleberry milkshake!"

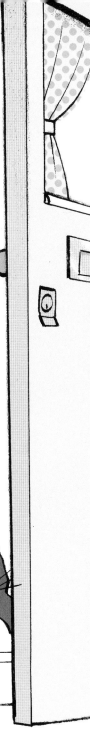

Chapter Two

The builders went as white as ghosts.

"Don't worry," said Pandora. "You don't *have* to have a milkshake. Come in!"

Slowly the builders edged inside, gaping at Granny. They'd never done building for a (*whisper it!*) witch before.

Granny gave them each a rock cake instead – which looked (and tasted) like *real* rocks!

"What are your names?" Pandora asked.

"I'm Bert," said the big one, crunching on his cake.

"Um," squeaked the small, guinea-pig one. "I'm Stanley."

The builders went out to unload their van. Granny watched, wand at the ready.

"That cement mixer looks jolly heavy," she said. "I could magic it in in a jif—"

"Uh uh!" cried Pandora, shaking her head. "Remember what Mum and Dad said."

"Oh," sighed Granny.

When the tools were unloaded, the building began. Pandora was very excited to watch. This room was to be her new bedroom!

But Granny was bored. It was all so slow! By lunchtime, the walls were still titchy.

"Let me help, Pip dear," Granny whispered at last, "or this room will take *forever*."

She whisked out her spell book. "Building spells are easy-peasy. I could whizz that room up in a flash."

"No," said Pandora. "Mum and Dad would find out and you'd get into trouble, Granny. We just can't."

But then, after lunch, Bert got a phone call. It was from his boss.

"Dave said we've made a mistake," Bert told Stanley. "We were meant to be at that *hotel* today, doing all those toilets!"

"What?" squeaked Stanley. "All a hundred and four?"

"Yep!"

Bert looked at Granny. "Sorry – got to go. And we can't come back until the toilets are all done."

"But that could take *weeks*," Granny groaned.

"What about my room?" cried Pandora. She'd been looking forward to her lovely new bedroom for *ages*.

Pandora and Granny exchanged glances. They were both thinking the same thing.

"Um … Granny," said Pandora slowly. "Do you think … we could – *carefully* – 'help' the builders finish my room before they go away?"

"Of course!" cried Granny. She'd been waiting for this all day!

She opened her spell book and flicked through the pages.

"OK," grinned Granny. "What shall it be? A sweet country cottage? A huge stately home? A cave-house? A lighthouse? A snazzy straw hut? Goodness, there's *so* much to choose from!"

BUILDING

"No, Granny – i-it's only a bedroom!" gasped Pandora. "Just a nice, plain room."

"Nonsense!" cried Granny. "Who wants a *plain* room when you can have something amazing? And wait! I've just found *the perfect thing*. Stand back!"

SPELLS, Part 1

Chapter Three

Granny waved her wand and the magic began.

The builders' tools sprang to life and started working all by themselves! Buckets grew legs and raced to the cement mixer, tossing water inside. Then spades started shovelling in heaps of sand.

"*Speedupio!*" Granny cried, and the mixer started whizzing round wildly.

Next an army of trowels dived into the mixer and flew out again loaded with cement. They slapped it on to bricks at breakneck speed – *fwip!*

"What sort of room am I having?" asked Pandora as the walls started shooting up around her.

"Ah ha!" grinned Granny. "Just you wait and see!"

Now saws started sawing, hammers started hammering and the walls towered up into a big, pointy cone.

"Look, Bert – she's done a *turret*!" squeaked Stanley.

"I know!" cried Bert. "Hey, wait a minute! I think she's building – *no* – she *can't* be."

But Pandora thought so, too…

"Hooray!" she cheered. "It's a castle! My favourite!"

Now Pandora pulled out *her* wand and magicked up some stained-glass windows. "Just like the castle in my princess book!" she smiled.

Next, they got to work on the furniture. Granny magicked up a four-poster bed with silky drapes and velvet cushions.

Then she did a dressing table with a
mirror in the shape
of a crown.

Pandora then made herself a big, golden
wardrobe filled with sparkly gowns. There
were rows of twinkly shoes and necklaces,
too.

Now Pandora's new bedroom was
finished!

"I love it!" she cried.

The builders packed away and jumped in the van. "Shame you can't help us with all those toilets!" grinned Bert.

Granny and Pandora waved them off. Then Granny magicked up some little roses around Pandora's window and popped a fluttering flag on top of the turret.

"Now then, Pandora," Granny said, "how about we put on our princess gowns?"

"Oh, yes!" beamed Pandora. But suddenly her bright smile faded.

"Um, Granny," she said. "Mum and Dad will be home soon. Do you think they'll, um … *like* my new bedroom?"

In the excitement she'd forgotten all about her parents' "no magic" rule. But they'd know in a flash that magic had been done.

"Of course they'll like it!" Granny nodded. "Who *wouldn't* want a castle on top of their garage, hmmm?!"

Chapter Four

Pandora was happily choosing her gown when suddenly her parents came home. It turned out they did *not* like the castle. Not one bit…

"It will have to go," Moonbeam sighed.

"Quite right!" Hugo spluttered. "The neighbours were … *staring*. Sorry, Pandora – but we *cannot* have a *castle* on our garage!"

Moonbeam said they'd have to get the

builders back first thing in the morning.

"But they've got a hundred and four toilets to do!" said Granny. She explained all about the big hotel. Hugo and Moonbeam frowned.

"Well, the castle's *got* to go!" they cried together.

Granny sighed. Poor Pandora. She loved her new bedroom so much! Then suddenly she had a really rather *magical* idea…

"Well," said Granny, "if something *must* be done, then maybe *I* could help?"

"You?" said Hugo.

"Me!" grinned Granny. "On the *outside* I could make Pandora's room look normal – but *inside* it would still be a *castle*. Then the neighbours wouldn't stare and Pandora would be happy!"

Pandora looked up.

"So my bed would be the same – and my wardrobe – and my mirror? And I'd still have a pointy turret ceiling?"

"Absolutely!" Granny smiled.

Pandora's parents exchanged looks. That meant m-a-g-i-c.

"Just this once?" Moonbeam whispered to Hugo.

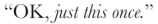

"OK, *just this once.*"

They hurried out and Granny pointed
her wand at the castle. Then she
uttered the magic spell…

"*Swippidy-dippidy, fiddle-dee-sticks
– inside castle – outside bricks!*"

POOF!

Pandora watched as a magical jet of mist billowed from the star on Granny's wand. It twinkled like glitter and smelled of blueberry muffins!

The sparkly mist hid everything from sight. But when it vanished, the *castle* had vanished, too! Now the room above the garage looked perfectly normal. Normal bricks, normal roof, normal everything.

Pandora raced inside to check her bedroom. Phew – it *still* looked like her beautiful castle! Everything – but everything – looked fit for a princess!

"Thanks, Granny," she beamed. "Clever you!"

Before Granny left, she had one more surprise. She waved her wand and…

WHIZZ! POP!

Now everyone found themselves in princess gowns. Even Pandora's dad!

"Hey!" shouted Hugo, as Granny jumped on her broomstick. "You can't leave until you put back my trousers!"

"Oh, princesses aren't meant to *shout*," grinned Granny. "Byeeeee!"

The Itchy WITCHY WEDDING!

Chapter One

"Pandora!" shrieked her mum. "Park at once – you're creasing your bridesmaid's dress! And I've told you *and* Granny no m-a-g-i-c at this wedding. It just leads to trouble – always!"

Pandora, who was zooming downstairs on her broomstick, parked it in the hall and climbed off.

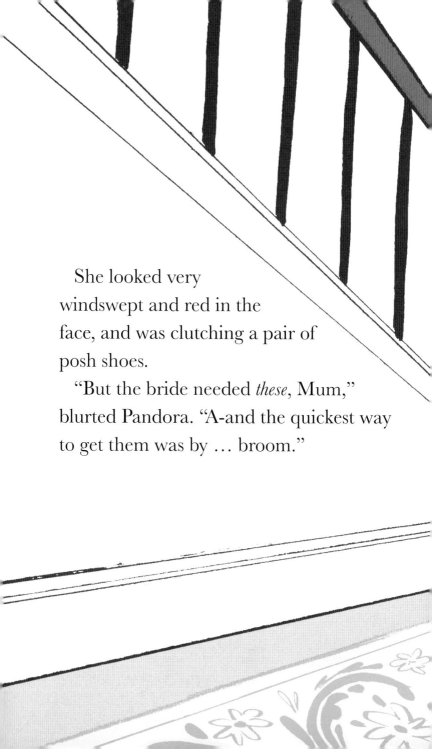

She looked very windswept and red in the face, and was clutching a pair of posh shoes.

"But the bride needed *these*, Mum," blurted Pandora. "A-and the quickest way to get them was by … broom."

Pandora liked helping. But this wedding was exhausting, and it hadn't even *started* yet!

How many times had she trekked up those stairs! The bride needed her veil, the bride needed her pearls, the bride needed her *sparkly shoes*!

"I only used my broomstick once," shrugged Pandora.

Her mother shook her head. "Well, no more!"

As Moonbeam hurried off, Pandora's cousin appeared. Primrose was a bridesmaid too. Uncle Teddy, the bridegroom, was *her* uncle, as well as Pandora's.

Primrose had never been a (*whisper it!*) witch, and never wanted to be. For one thing, witches had messy hair and Primrose loved her shiny curls so much.

Primrose took the shoes from Pandora's hands and trotted off to find Annabelle, the bride.

"Hey," frowned Pandora. "I was doing that."

"Why not brush your hair instead?" called back Primrose. "Not that it could *ever* be as shiny as mine."

"What do you mean!" muttered Pandora, peering into the mirror. "Anyway, our hair's not even been *done* yet! I'll look fine when the hairdresser's finished with me!"

Primrose disappeared through a door leaving Pandora alone. Where *was* the hairdresser anyway?

Pandora decided she'd better go and ask her mum.

Moonbeam was in the lounge with a worried-looking bride whose feet wouldn't fit in her shoes.

"Mum…" said Pandora.

"Pandora – hold on."

"But, Mum…"

"Pandora – please wait!"

"*But the hairdresser!*" cried Pandora. "*He's really late!*"

"Oh no!" shrieked the bride. "She's right – he's not coming!"

"Lucky *I'm* here then!" came a cheery voice, as Granny zoomed down the chimney on her broomstick.

A big cloud of soot billowed out behind her, turning everything smoky grey – the bride's pearly necklace, her floaty white dress, her slightly "too small now" shoes.

"I'm perfectly splendid at hairstyles!" grinned Granny. "OK, who's first?"

Chapter Two

"Never mind our *hair*," sniffled the bride. "Look at my *dress*, it's ruined!" Tears burst from her eyes as she rubbed at the dusty grey soot.

"Oh, I can fix that, dear!" Granny smiled. She looked at Moonbeam, who nodded. Magic was the only way to get everyone clean in time.

Granny waved her wand and the soot

disappeared. But the bride gave *another* big sniff.

Her floaty white dress was now straight and electric blue, and was dotted with cats and broomsticks! On her head was a pointy witch's hat.

"Eeee!" she squeaked as a spider dropped down.

"Ta daa!" beamed Granny. "A *much* nicer outfit for a bride!"

Moonbeam, however, didn't look happy. "See what happens when I let you do magic!" she cried.

"But *do* let her put me right!" blubbered Annabelle. "Please!"

Moonbeam agreed, so Granny turned
her back to normal. And now it was time to
do their hair.

With another small wand-flick
the lounge became a hairdresser's
with sparkly mirrors,
sinks and sprays.

"No, Mum!" yelled Moonbeam. "Put the wand away! You must style our hair without it."

Granny gave a gulp.

"Don't worry," said Pandora. "You'll be fine."

But, without magic, Granny was not fine. She brushed and she sprayed but not one single hair would go right.

"I'm not going out like this!" shrieked
Primrose, and the bride started crying
again.

"All right," groaned Moonbeam.
"Magical hairstyles it is!" She turned to
Granny. "But don't go wild."

"Me? Go wild, dear?" Granny twinkled.
"As if!"

In the blink of an eye, her spell book was out and magic filled the air. Scissors were snipping, tongs were twirling and sprays were spritzing like crazy. Granny finished with a dusting of magical stars…

"Perfect!"

Everyone gasped. What had Granny done? Pandora's bun looked like a tree – home to hundreds of *bats*. Moonbeam's hair was a sea of curls, with mermaids and a wriggly octopus.

As for Primrose, her shiny ponytail now had a *pony* attached too! And the bride wore a fairytale castle on her head, complete with a trickling fountain!

"MUM!" bellowed Moonbeam.

"What?" Granny shrugged. "It's lovely!"

Meanwhile, Pandora had found a hair magazine. She showed Granny some "normal" wedding hairstyles.

"Oh, all right then…" sighed Granny. "If you're sure."

She waved her wand and with a small PING, everyone's hair looked just right!

"Phew!" puffed Moonbeam. "Now, wand away, please."

"Mum!" cried Pandora, peeping through the window. "The wedding cars are here! Time to go!"

Chapter
Three

Two smart cars were waiting in the street
to drive them to the wedding in a castle
nearby.

Granny, Moonbeam and the two
bridesmaids got into the front car.
Annabelle was leaving ten minutes later in
the other car with her dad.

"Stop scratching your head, Pandora,"
said Moonbeam as the car set off down the

road.

"But it's really itchy," Pandora frowned.

"It must be that hairspray I used…" muttered Granny.

"Well, *my* head's not itching," said Primrose, stroking her curls.

They arrived at the castle and waited for the bride, who got there right on time. But as she wriggled out of the car – *ripppp!*

The heel of her shoe had caught in her veil and had made a jolly big hole.

"Oh n-n-no!" sniffled Annabelle. "*What shall we do?*"

"Don't worry!" cried Granny, and before they could stop her, the hole was magically mended. Except Granny had used a *cobweb* stitch – her favourite!

Moonbeam rolled her eyes.

"You don't *like* it?" sighed Granny.

"I do!" Pandora chipped in.

"Mum," groaned
Moonbeam. "*Not again.*"

Shrugging, Granny magicked the cobweb away. Then Moonbeam whisked her into the castle where all the other guests were waiting.

The music started and Annabelle's dad led her in and down the aisle. Behind them walked the bridesmaids but Granny saw that Pandora was still scratching her head. And now the *bride* was scratching *hers* too.

"Don't *ever* use that hairspray again!" whispered Moonbeam, and Granny blushed.

After the wedding it was time for the feast in the summer house down by the lake. Pandora's dad, Hugo, dashed on ahead to check that everything was in place. The bridesmaids went too, along with Granny (who liked helping!).

The summer house was filled with garlands of flowers and rows of lacy bunting. There were neatly cut sandwiches, gleaming iced cakes and bottles of sparkly champagne.

Hugo checked everything. "All in order!" he smiled. But suddenly he noticed that the top of the wedding cake was missing a small bride and groom made from fondant icing.

He hurried away to find the chef but no sooner had he gone than Granny whisked out her wand.

"Right – let's pretty things up!" she cried, and she uttered a magical makeover spell…

Beetle juice and bunting-bats,
spider cakes and crispy cats.
Cobweb trifle, sugar mice – fill
this room with all things nice!

BANG!

And suddenly the place was filled with Granny's favourite things – crisps in the shape of little cats, trifles thick with dust, and rows of batty bunting *which flapped*.

"What?!" spluttered Hugo as he walked back in.

"Granny!"

Chapter Four

"I was just twinkling things up a bit," said Granny.

"Well!" gasped Hugo. "Put it right!"

Granny looked most disappointed but did as she was told. Just in time too, for at that moment the bride and groom walked in. And behind them came a string of guests – men in smart suits and ladies in big, fancy hats.

When Moonbeam appeared she looked hot and bothered. Her hat was making her head itch like mad. Or it might be that silly hairspray Granny had used...

Smart waiters now brought round the wedding food.

"I much preferred my catty crisps!" sniffed Granny as she nibbled a perfectly neat (but *boring*) cucumber sandwich.

Finally, everyone gave a huge cheer as the bride and groom cut the wedding cake. But suddenly…

"Arggh!" Annabelle screamed as her eyes were drawn to the top of it.

Instead of the fondant bride and groom, there were two big, hairy spiders. One was wearing a top hat and tails, and the other wore a veil and was holding a bunch of thistles.

"Surprise!" piped up Granny. "We lost the decoration so I thought you might like to borrow Sam and Sabrina instead!"

And Granny's pet spiders weren't the only surprise. As the grown-ups sipped their champagne they discovered it *wasn't* champagne at all but a sludgy dark-blue drink.

"Beetles????!!!" boomed a man, as three shiny black ones scuttled out of his glass.

"But of course!" grinned Granny. "It's my beetlecurrant fizz! Aren't you lucky I forgot to turn it back to champagne!"

After that, Hugo made doubly sure that Granny kept her hands *off* her wand. Moonbeam, Pandora *and* the bride were all still scratching their heads, and the beetlecurrant man looked most unwell!

"Your granny's nothing but trouble," whispered Primrose.

"She was only trying to help!" Pandora frowned.

Now it was time for some photographs. The photographer took everyone out to the lake and arranged them in a group. But Primrose, who was next to Pandora, was now scratching *her* head too.

"Eeeee!" she cried, as her shiny curls flew about.

Then Pandora noticed that *everyone* was scratching. So it *couldn't* be the hairspray…

"Hold still!" cried the photographer as they jiggled about. "What ... what's *wrong* with you all?!"

But it was Pandora who worked it out, just as the camera went CLICK!

"Eeek!" she squeaked. Oh no – they all had … *nits!!!*

With a gulp, she slipped off to Granny and whispered in her ear. Nodding, Granny waved her wand and – POOF – the nits were all vanished away! Then everyone stopped scratching and went in for the dancing. Hooray!

"*Thanks, Granny*," whispered Pandora. Her magic had saved the day. Now no one would ever know about the "uninvited" wedding guests.

"Lucky those nits are all gone," smiled Pandora.

Or were they…?

The End